Gran's Gang go to Spain

To Katie & Austen

Best Wishes

Adrian Townsend

ADRIAN TOWNSEND

Gran's Gang go to Spain

Illustrated by Kate Chesterton

First Published 2002 by
Grassy Hill Publishing
52 Wheatley Road, Garsington, Oxford, OX44 9ER

ISBN 1-903569-05-2

To Eileen, Robin, Marie and Nigel.
Life Members of Club Nautico

Read this first

If you haven't read *Gran's Gang* and
don't know much about Ada and her
friends why not turn to page 154 to get
to know them first.

Contents

Contents

Getting Ready

My Gran's in trouble AGAIN.

She and my mum were seen on T.V. and Gran showed her orange knickers to the camera. There was a big iron mark on the bum. Mum was embarrassed, now mum's not talking to her. All the people in our street saw Gran on T.V. They thought she was great. They even ask for her autograph.

Only the milkman teases her. He says he could 'iron out her difficulties' but Gran ignores him.

The rest of Gran's Gang; Ethel, Winnie and Nora are famous as well now. Ethel got new sponsorship for her banger racing. Now she's 'Unethical Ethel sponsored by Crystalene Oil 'Slicker than Most.' Nora got a pay rise from the people whose office she cleans. "I never knew you worked so fast," said the boss and he gave her a new apron with the company logo on. "Wear it when you're next on TV," he said. Winnie's ladies basketball team now get loads more people to watch their home basketball games. "They

come to watch my dribbling skills,"
says Winnie.

So Gran and her gang are happy. It's
just mum. She can't see the funny side
of what happened at the night club.
"I've been humiliated. I can't show my
face in the street. People are laughing at
me. What did I do to deserve your
Gran?" she said to me.
"You're her daughter," I said back to
her, but she glowered so I said no more.

It was Donna from next who helped
mum get over things. She took mum to
a Rustlers concert; my mum's second

favourite pop group. Afterwards Donna told Mum how lucky she was to have Gran. She said mum should look on the bright side.

Mum cheered up a bit. Donna told her that she and Gran 'just needed to bond together'. She said mum and Gran should go on holiday together. Donna offered to look after me for a week. Mum agreed.

"I could do with a break and some sunshine," she said.

"I'll take your Gran to Spain."

That was the beginning of more trouble.

Gran was ironing a new clubbing top
when mum went round to see her. She
couldn't believe it when mum
suggested a holiday in Spain. Gran's

never been 'abroad' before. After thinking about it for a few days and typing the words *Spain*, *Clubbing* and *Dancing* into the Internet she rang mum to say she was 'Up for it!'

Next day mum and Gran went to the travel agents. A young man called Colin typed some words into a computer.

SEA VIEW

ENSUITE

POOL SIDE BAR

DISCO

Mum frowned, Gran smiled. Colin typed again.

DAILY MEAL PLAN

PIANO LOUNGE

QUIET AND RELAXING

Mum smiled Gran frowned. "What about this?" asked Colin.

SPACIOUS AND COMFORTABLE

GOOD ENTERTAINMENT

SOMETHING FOR EVERYONE

They both nodded.

"Right now," said Colin. "One week Hotel Ambassador, St Fernoux, Costa Brava, Spain.

  2 PEOPLE

  EN-SUITE

  SEA VIEW

  MEAL PLAN

  plus insurance."

"That's just £374.24 each for the week."

"What!" said Gran and Mum together.

"You said it was around £250."

"Oh yes," said Colin. "That was before the extras."

"We can't afford that," said Gran.

"Sorry we'll have to leave it," said mum.

And they got up to leave.

Colin could see he was about to lose a sale.

"Hang on ladies, let me play with the figures, let me see what I can do." And he began to type at his computer again.

"Here we go, here we go," he said.

"Without the sea view and one or two other bits and pieces I can get it down to £325. Now there's a bargain."

"Not in my book," said Gran.

"Nor mine," said mum. "Is there nothing cheaper?"

"Afraid not," said Colin. "The only way you could go cheaper is if you were in a group of twenty. Then you could get group discount and you two could both go for free."

Mum and Gran looked at each other.

"Let's do it. Let's find nine other people each," said Gran.

"Deal," said mum and she shook Gran's hand.

Mum and Gran only had two days to get nine people each. Colin said he could hold the booking until the weekend.

Gran started straight away, she went round to Nora's. Nora was in the back garden, roller blading down a small practice ramp. Gran told her about the holiday and Nora agreed to go.

"I could do with a break from cleaning."

Ethel didn't need much persuading either. She loves "sea and sand" as she put it. She said it would be good to get away from Basil and Betty Wainwright who live next door. Gran didn't tell Ethel she'd already asked them. She needed them to make up the numbers.

"What a good idea," said Basil Wainwright. "There's not much doing in the garden at the moment. A week away would be lovely wouldn't it?" he said to Mrs Wainwright.

"A week away from her next door." And he pointed at Ethel, who they could all see in her garage. "She's been revving that engine for the last two hours."

"Oh lovely!" said Mrs Wainwright. "You count us in Ada and thank you for thinking of us."

Winnie was more difficult to persuade. She was worried about

missing an important basketball match.
"I can't go," she said. They'll put
Miriam Young in the team in my place.
"Oh no they won't," said Gran. "She's
gone to Australia for three months. I
met your team manager this morning
and he said she'd be out of the team for
the whole season."

That clinched it for Winnie. Now she
could go on holiday with the Gang and
still be in the basketball team when she
came back.
"Right, that makes six then," said Gran.
She was counting up the numbers with

Nora. "The Gang plus the Wainwrights but don't tell Ethel about them yet."

"You still need another four Ada," said Nora. "What about Harry Thistlethwaite? I'm sure he'd go. I'm seeing him later. I'll ask him."

"OK," said Gran. "And we could ask June and Bob Yates. They seem to be taking lots of holidays since Bob's retired. He's a 'new man' now he's not working at the undertakers. He'll be fun."

"Just one more then," said Nora and they both sat and thought in silence. They couldn't think of anyone else.

Eventually Nora looked at Gran. "The Vicar's not too bad, and sometimes I think he's a bit lonely. He could do with a holiday."

"Not likely," said Gran. "He'd talk about cream cakes and good works all the time. No I'm not asking him. We'd have to be desperate."

There was more silence.

"I think we are," said Nora.

* * *

Mum was getting desperate too. Finding nine friends to go on holiday was much more difficult. Mum's not

like Gran, she stays in and reads a lot. All her old friends from school have moved away and she only talks to them on the phone.

It was Donna who sorted it out. She got her sister and her husband to go and she persuaded Mary Whitefleet that there was a church trip to Spain. Donna said the Vicar was going and he needed a hand. Later she asked her driving instructor, Wally Coulter of Wally's Wheels Driving School. He said he'd go and play some golf.

Mum got two 'friends' from her

reading club; Robert and Rita Rodgers and she mentioned the trip to 'Young Gary' our window cleaner. He said he and his girlfriend needed a holiday.

There was only one place left to fill and Donna seized her chance. She was meant to be looking after me, but she rally, really wanted to go.

Eventually after the promise of two new CDs, a trip to the cinema and a new pair of trainers I "agreed" to stay with my auntie Joan for a week. Muesli for breakfast and old fashioned blankets for a week, Ugh!

Two days later, after picking up the tickets, mum asked me to check the list of people going to Spain with her. There was mum, Donna, Young Gary, his girlfriend, Wally Coulter, The Rodgers, Mary Whitefleet, The Vicar, Donna's sister and her husband, June and Bob Yates, Basil and Betty Wainwright, Harry Thistlethwaite, Nora, Winnie, Ethel and Gran.

When I'd finished reading out the names she looked up and said,

"What have I done?"

The day of departure arrived. Mum and
19 'oddballs' were off to St.Fernoux,
Costa Brava, Spain.

Harry Thistlethwaite had insisted that he should drive the Holiday Special coach to the airport. Gran and the Gang were the first ones waiting to get on. They took up most of the pavement with all the luggage they were taking. Ethel was really happy singing, "We're off to sunny Spain." Then she saw the Wainwrights struggling along the pavement with suitcases. "Where are you two off? Have you been stealing garden gnomes in those suitcases?"

"No we haven't," said Basil Wainwright "We're having a break from you."

"We're going to exotic parts," said Betty.

"St. Fernoux, Spain." said Basil. "A week with our friends, away from you."

"Oh no you're not." said Ethel. "I'm going with Ada and the Gang and you're not coming. I checked, I checked," and she turned to Gran who

wasn't there. She'd suddenly forgotten something inside her house.

Well, the journey to the airport was quiet except for Harry singing to himself. Basil and Betty sat at the front of the coach, Betty snivelling and Basil muttering about wasting money. Ethel sat sulking at the back.

She didn't cheer up until she got to the airport and everyone had to walk through a special archway to see if they were hiding metal objects. Basil Wainwright walked through and the alarm kept going off and he kept being

sent through again.

"Have you put your keys and coins in the tray?" said the security guard.

"Yes I have," said Basil "I can't understand it."

"Oh dear," said Betty.

Six times Basil went through and he got really flustered.

"It's those iron tablets you took this morning," said Betty.

"Don't be silly," said Basil, going red.

"Or it's those fillings in your teeth," Betty continued. Basil looked like he was going to explode.

"Lord save us and Preserve us," said the Vicar.

"Amen," said Mary Whitefleet.

Finally Basil went through without a bleep. Gran was relieved. She'd been trying not to laugh. It was Ethel who broke the awkward silence.

"Bad luck Basil," she said. "I thought you were done for there. It must have been your nuts and bolts. I always knew you had a screw loose!"

Everyone burst out laughing, even Mary Whitefleet smiled.

On the plane everyone relaxed even

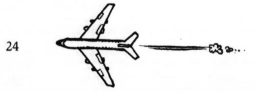

more. Nora said she'd like to have jet engines on her roller blades. Winnie said she'd like to be a stewardess with a lovely uniform. Mum sucked sweets and held onto the seat and Betty and Basil were delighted. They were moved up to Club Class because there wasn't enough seats in economy.

"Careful grooming and good manners always pays off," she later said to Harry Thistlethwaite.

Gran's Gang holiday package arrived safely in Spain.

* * *

Most of the first day was spent getting to know the hotel. Nora and Winnie wandered around to see 'what was on offer.' Two large bars, two restaurants, a fitness suit, swimming pool, games room, children's area, disco and beauty parlour plus sauna.

"Oh I've never tried one of those," said Winnie "I must go in there."

Mum and Donna were sharing a room together. It was quite big with a balcony but by the time mum had unpacked all her reading books it seemed a lot smaller.

"You really must get out more," Donna said to mum. "We're on holiday you know, not back at school."

Mum laughed and nodded but she did point out that their en-suite bathroom was now full to overflowing with Donna's make up and beauty treatments.

"Every little helps," said Donna, then they both bounced on their beds and stuffed themselves with free chocolate provided by the hotel. It had been a long day but Gran's Gang were in Spain at last.

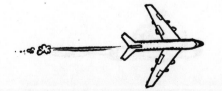

Nora's Costa Fortune

After the journey to Spain most people were tired and went to bed early. Next morning they began to drift down to breakfast and help themselves to the sort of food they don't usually eat at home. Basil Wainwright had yoghurt with fresh fruit. Mary Whitefleet had 'very thin' ham and a hard boiled egg. The vicar was adventurous. He had bread covered in chocolate drops and a large mug of frothy chocolate.

"The Lord knows how to keep me

sweet," he said to mum and Donna as they walked into breakfast.

"Ugh, not more chocolate!" said Donna.

Mum and Donna had finished all the free hotel chocolate and a big bar of duty free they had bought at the airport. They didn't feel like more for breakfast.

"Where's your mum?" asked Donna looking around the room to see who was in for breakfast.

"Oh she won't be up yet," said mum. "It's far too early for her. That's the trouble. With all her clubbing, she gets to bed far too late then doesn't get up

till nearly dinner time."

Nora and Winnie were already up. In fact they'd been up since 6 o'clock. They were sharing a room together because Nora is always up early for her job and Winnie gets up early at home to start basketball training. Nora had woken as usual at 5:30 and at 6 am when she saw Winnie was awake had suggested they go for a walk in the town to see what St. Fernoux is like.

They left the hotel and walked down a quiet narrow street with tall buildings and little verandas sticking out of the

upstairs windows. After several winding streets they came to a large open area with shops around a large central square with trees and places to sit and café chairs piled up ready to be laid out.

"This is nice," said Nora.

"Yes," Winnie agreed.

Some men were on ladders putting up lots of white paper decorations around the trees and lamp posts. Others had coloured lights.

"It's like Christmas in summer," said Winnie.

A Spanish man saw them and smiled.

"Fiesta - Fiesta de belleza", he said.

Winnie and Nora smiled. They walked through the square and suddenly found themselves on the sea front.

"Wow," said Nora "This is nice."

Winnie agreed.

St. Fernoux had a beautiful sea front with lots of large shops and hotels set against hills and mountains behind. In front, over a road was the beach. It was enormous with yellow sand curving all the way around the bay, it went on forever. Beyond the sand was a deep

blue sea. It was early in the morning and only a few people were on the beach.

"Let's go for a paddle," said Winnie. "We can tell Ada we've dipped our toes in the Mediterranean before she's even had breakfast."

They both rushed across the road and on to the beach. Nora stopped to take her shoes off.

"Race you to the sea," she said and started running towards the water.

Winnie wasn't going to be beaten in a race with an over weight office cleaner,

she was the athlete of the Gang. She
ripped off her shoes and raced after
Nora, catching up with her easily. They
were both level with each other when
suddenly they heard someone shout.

"Atencion !"

They stopped suddenly and noticed
they were standing on a hard road
exactly the same colour as the sand.

The voice from nowhere shouted
again and then a whirling blue and
white shape circled around them before
coming to a stop. "No paseo," said the
shape. Nora and Winnie now stood next

to a young man in a white vest and blue

shorts. He was wearing elbow pads,

knee pads and roller blades. "No paseo,"
he said.

"Sorry we're English we don't
understand," said Nora.

"Ah Englees."

"I'm sorry I did not see you," he said in
good English.

"I did not expect to see anyone on the
beach track so early."

"The beach track?" said Winnie.

"Yes," said the man. "You are on the
beach track; it's built for cyclists roller
bladers and boarders. It's for fun but it's
also a quick way from one end of town

to the other."

Nora and Winnie looked along the track. Now they could see it went all the way across the sand linking the square they had walked through to another park at the far end of the bay.

"We call it our roller track. In Spain we like to have fun on the beach. Good morning I'm José."

Nora's eyes were now very wide.

"Oh I like to have fun too," said Winnie, looking José up and down.

"And me," said Nora. She looked at the long, smooth roller-blading road.

"José, can anyone use this track?" asked Nora.

"Oh yes," said José, "But you must have wheels; bikes, boards or rollers. No walking!" laughed José and he was just about to push off when Nora grabbed him by the vest.

"Sorry to stop you, but I noticed you're wearing *Licom Super Gliders*, they're amazing aren't they?"

José looked down at his roller blades. "Oh yes," he said. "Very good for speed. You know about them?"

"A little," said Nora, "I can do a bit of

roller blading myself."

"Can you really?" said José. "Then you must come and join our club. We meet everyday at 4 o'clock in the Plaza de héroe and he pointed to the square Nora and Winnie had just walked through. "See you later," said José as he glided backwards before moving off at speed.

Nora was so excited about joining what she called 'Proper Roller Blading' that she didn't eat much breakfast when she got back to the hotel. She didn't tell anyone else about meeting

José or the roller blade track.

"They'll only laugh at me," she said to Winnie and she made Winnie promise not to say anything. Winnie agreed to keep quiet and go with Nora later that afternoon to meet José.

"José the hunk," she called him.

They both spent a quiet morning by the pool. Mum was there as well. She put a stack of books under a sun bed and covered herself with sun cream, a hat and a towel over her body to stop herself from getting prickly heat.

"She looked like she was in a hospital

not sun bathing," said Gran.

At 4 o'clock Nora and Winnie went to
meet José. Nora decided to wear an old
tracksuit and her working hat. "For a bit
of protection if I come a cropper."

Winnie wore her latest bikini top and

her new tight peddle pusher shorts.

"Skimpy," Nora called them.

"José won't mind," said Winnie.

They walked towards the square together. 'Like Laurel and Hardy' my mum said later.

When they got to the Plaza de héroe, José was already there. He was surprised to see them again but came to greet them.

"Laydees, English Laydees," he said. "I didn't think you would come. So you want to use the track. That's OK, it's free. You just need wheels."

Nora hadn't brought her roller blades
to Spain and she wondered if she'd got
enough money to buy some new ones -
she so desperately wanted to try the
track.

José could see Nora looked worried.
"Don't worry," he said. "I'll lend you
some. Do you want blades or a board?"
"Oh, I've never done any boarding," said
Nora. "No. I'll stick to what I know."

José whistled through his fingers and
lots of other young men stopped and
looked at him. He said a lot in Spanish
and then a pair of roller blades was

passed to Nora. Winnie was introduced to Pedro, who offered her a skate board. "Oh, I'm not sure," she said. "Perhaps if you teach me," and she took Pedro's hand and led him to a nearby café.

Nora couldn't wait to get started. She strapped her borrowed roller blades on and did a short circuit with a pirouette before returning back to where she started. The young men clapped and whistled.

"Número Uno, brillante," said Pedro.

Nora smiled.

"Well," said José. "The English laydee

can blade. Let's take a trip down the track."

Nora followed José and the rest of 'the boys' as she called them, out of the square onto the sand-coloured track across the beach.

They got faster and faster and Nora kept up with them. Each time they did a particular arm movement she did the same. As she sped across the sunny beach she enjoyed the smell of the sea, the sun and the company. Nora was the middle carriage in a long roller blading train making its way across the sands of

St Fernoux.

José caught the mood of what was going on. He started to perform new movements. Each time he did everyone copied him including Nora. She managed twisting turns, hooplas, up and downs, one foot gliders, squat backwards and Spanish Spring. When they all arrived at the other side of the beach everyone gathered around and patted Nora on the back.

"Hey go for it Nora," said Pedro.

"Yeah crazy ladyee," said Juan.

Nora was puffing and blowing, but

was very pleased with herself.

"Thanks for letting me join in boys,"

she said. "I feel like I'm in a new gang."

"You are," said Pedro. "We are the

Costa Bravo Gang and you must join us.

But it's not easy there is a problem."

"What's wrong?" asked Nora.

"Well," said José "We would like to give

you the badge of the Costa Bravo," and

he pointed to a gold medallion that

everyone was wearing. "But it's not

easy, we cannot ... and it's a bit

embarrassing ... you see you have to

earn it ... and it involves having some

fun with the foreign tourists," and he
pointed to the people on the beach. He
took a deep breath. "Nora if you want
to earn the Costa Bravo Badge you have
to make three separate, timed runs
along the beach track and do as we say.
You have to pass a test. Do you want to
do it?"

"Oh I do," said Nora "I do."

Ten minutes later Nora was ready and
waiting at one end of the beach track.
She had borrowed a pair of dark
sunglasses and a baseball cap and was
ready for:

Test number one: The Tourist Slalom.

Nora pushed off gently. She had to keep gliding until she saw a group of people ready to cross the roller bladers' track. Then she had to circle all the way around them and return. If she touched any of them or there was an accident she would not pass the test.

Nora glided slowly waiting for her victims. In the distance, four people got up from the beach and shook their towels. They were ready to leave the beach. Nora accelerated. The group approached the track. They didn't see

her coming. Nora sped towards them.
She heard English voices and odd
words, sermon, windows, bikini and
cakes. It was Young Gary, his girlfriend,
Mary Whitefleet and the Vicar.

'Mary, you've done it again,' said Nora to herself, as she sped towards them. She went around the front of them as they stepped onto the road and around the back as they stepped off. Mary nearly dropped her sun hat but held onto it just in time.

"Goodness me, what was that?" said the Vicar.

"Local youths," said Young Gary.

"Disgraceful," said Mary Whitefleet.

"Brilliant," said Nora to herself. She had passed the first test.

Test number two: Jump the Whales

José explained that the local people called sun bathing tourists 'beached whales' because they look like pink whales as they lie sunbathing.

"St Fernoux has a lot of old... retired visitors," explained José. "Anyway, test number two is to pick a 'beached whale' and jump over it. You can jump off the track onto the sand but you mustn't fall over or touch the whale. You must be back on the track, roller blading away before the whale sits up."

Nora was worried by this test. She

was good on her roller blades but her knees were a bit 'suspect' for jumping. I'm no Spring Chicken, she thought to herself. Slightly nervous she looked around for a 'beached whale' close to the roller blade track. She picked one out not too far away. She'd give it a go. Off she went, slowly at first, she had to get her speed right or the jump wouldn't work. As she got close to her whale she could see it had a lot of hair in a net. Her whale was bright pink with a blue hair net. It was Betty Wainwright. Nora was already on her

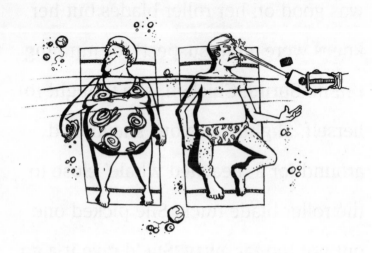

approach, she couldn't stop now. On
she went then weeeeee ... the take off.
Nora saw it all in slow motion. Over
Betty's pink tummy, over her
outstretched arm, over her packet of
mint balls and down onto the sand. Oh
no! Not the sand, onto a tube of sun

cream. Nora tried to miss it but could not. She landed on the sun cream; a long white jet of cream flew through the air landing on Basil Wainwright's nose. Nora braced herself for the landing. She wobbled. Her knees creaked but she stayed upright. She ran along the sand back to the roller blade track. She'd done it. Test number two was in the bag.

So was Basil Wainwright, he rummaged through his beach bag muttering about "blooming Spanish seagulls."

Test number three: Spanish Sprinkle

Nora was now completely shattered. She had a long sit down with the rest of the Costa Bravo Gang and a large drink of water. José told her how good she was and that the final test was really quite easy.

"All you have to do," he said, handing her a full bottle of sparkling water, "is glide past the beach whales and spray them with water. You must get six to sit up so they think it's raining."

Everyone looked up at the bright blue sky and laughed and said something

about English and rain.

"Shake the bottle before you spray," said José. "Good luck."

Nora took one last drink of her own water before setting off. This run did not need a lot of energy but it did need some luck. Nora could see a large group of 'whales' lying close to the track, she headed towards them. She shook the fizzy water. With one finger over the end she sprayed the group. The first whale got really wet and sat up quickly followed by numbers two, three and four. Numbers five and six were Donna

and my mum. Donna touched her tummy. "Water?" she said to herself and sat up as well. But mum was asleep. She had an open book lying on her face. It had stopped her feeling the water. In fact mum was having a lovely dream about Billy Jay and dancing and shirts and ironing and yellow and my Gran and roller blades. "Oh no!" shouted mum in her sleep. Then she suddenly sat bolt upright. "Oh no," she said. "Oh no!"

"Don't worry," said Donna "It's only a couple of spots of rain."

Nora was ecstatic. She'd passed the final test. She glided back to the others. They clapped and cheered and chanted. "Bravo Nora, Bravo Nora." They lifted her on to a low wall and placed the gold medallion around her neck.

Costa Bravo Nora!

Ada's Leather Trousers

My mum was really beginning to enjoy the holiday. No cooking, no washing up, plenty of sun and relaxing. Even Gran was quiet. That was the trouble.

A couple of days into the holiday and Gran was not happy.

"Why did I sign up for this?" she said to Ethel. "When I looked on the Internet it said Spain was full of clubs and disco places. This place is **D**ull with a capital **D**."

St Fernoux is, in truth, a bit on the

quiet side and mum hadn't been completely honest with Gran when she read a Spanish guide book about it. What really set Gran in a bad mood was when she saw the hotel name. In the English brochure it's called Hotel Ambassador. In Spain, there's a big sign at the front that says Hotel Geriatrica.

"Good grief," said Gran when she first saw it. "I'm not staying here. She wants me to stay in an old folk's home." Gran calmed down when the hotel manager said it was "just a language thing," but it started Gran's bad mood.

Gran spent the first two nights of the holiday looking for clubs in the town. Nothing. Plenty of bars, shops, restaurants and cinemas but no clubs. She thought she'd struck lucky when she found a large Spanish building called 'Club Nautico'. She went inside expecting doormen, bright lights and club music. What she got was a lot of old people singing songs about the sea and taking turns on a stage to perform traditional Spanish sea songs.

"I knew we should have gone to Ibiza," said Gran.

On the third day of the holiday mum was beginning to feel really guilty for tricking Gran, so she suggested that she and Gran should go shopping for some new clubbing gear. Gran had spotted that St. Fernoux did have some "seriously good" clothes shop.

"We can have a meal and take in some entertainment," said Mum.

"Entertainment," said Gran. "What did you have in mind? Bingo at the Club Nautico!"

Mum ignored Gran's last remark and they agreed to give shopping a try.

Come five o'clock, word of the shopping trip had got round and Mum and Gran were joined by Donna, Ethel, Nora and Winnie. "Oh dear!" thought Mum.

They set off in two groups of three and pretty soon were in the centre of town 'popping' in and out of the different clothes shops. At first Gran was still in a bad mood "It's well made stuff but it's all so old fashioned." Mum kept quiet and hoped things would improve. They did.

In the third shop they visited, Winnie

had seen a nice pair of beach shorts and wanted to try them on. Mum, Gran and Donna waited while Ethel, Winnie, Nora and the shop assistant discussed sizes. The trouble was the shop assistant didn't speak English. Nora, Winnie and Ethel were shouting out numbers; ten - twelve - fourteen.

"No I'm not!"

"I bet you wish you were."

"No that's American size."

"This is European size."

"Well I've never been a twenty six in my life!"

The shop assistant did her best but didn't seem to want to sell the shorts - she kept trying to pull them away from Winnie. "No nino. No nino," she kept saying.

"I'm not a nine. There isn't a size nine" said Winnie. "I know what size I am."

Eventually the shop assistant let go of the shorts and with a shrug of her shoulders and a very loud "Ooh, la, la." ushered Winnie into a changing room.

Everyone waited as Winnie disappeared behind a swinging door. They could see the top of Winnie's hair

above the door and Winnie's ankles and feet below.

My Mum said what followed was "Better than watching T.V."

First Winnie got her head stuck in her own jumper as she tried to take it off. "Oh Ethel I'm stuck, my elbow's caught on the hanger. Can you give me a hand? I can't get my arm up it's stuck on the... Oh thanks."

Ethel had gone over to the door and pulled Winnie's jumper up by reaching over the top of the swinging door. "Watch my hair don't ..."

"Steady."

"Mind my perm. Watch the perm. Oh that's better." Ethel returned to the group holding Winnie's jumper.

Mum and Donna were trying not to laugh when Nora said "What's she up to now?"

Everyone looked back to the swinging door. Through the gap at the bottom they could see the new shorts around Winnie's ankles and then Winnie's arms appeared as she tried to pull them up. This was followed by a loud bang on the door and a cry of "Ouch! Oh no!

My perm!" Winnie had hit her head on the door as she bent down. Seconds later Winnie's ankles, still with the new shorts around them appeared through the bottom of the door as Winnie's head disappeared from the top. Then there was a loud bump as she sat on the floor.

Donna burst out laughing and had to hide behind a display of hair products. The assistant looked worried so Ethel went and peered under the door.

"Are you alright Winnie? You're causing a bit of a commotion. Do you want a hand?"

"No," shrieked Winnie. "I'll get these shorts on if it's the last thing I..." RIP.

There was an enormous ripping sound and the whole shop fell silent. The shop assistant looked really worried. Mum looked at her feet and Donna crept to the door of the shop. "Oh err..." could be heard from behind the cubicle door, then more rustling of clothes. Eventually Winnie emerged from the changing room looking flustered and with her hair to one side. Her skirt was on back to front.

She handed the shorts to the shop

assistant who examined them very carefully but couldn't find a tear or rip.

"I've decided not to take them." Winnie said in a suddenly very posh voice. "They're not my style. I'm more used to designer

clothing," she said and holding her hand to her waist started to limp out of the shop. "Have you got a safety pin?" she said to Nora, "I really need one."

After Winnie's performance in the last shop, mum suggested they split up into two's instead of going everywhere together. Everyone agreed to meet up later, when they had all done their shopping. "We can meet at 9 o'clock outside that big building by the beach. You know that blue and green one; Club Nautico it's called."

Mum wanted to keep an eye on Gran

so she took her off down a twisting little side street. It was there that Gran saw the leather shop: 'Cuero St. Fernoux.' Gran had always wanted some leather gear for clubbing and she had read on the internet that leather clothing was 'a very good buy' in Spain.

"Oh let's go in and have a look," she said to mum and before mum could say anything Gran was half way in.

Inside it smelt of shoes and wallets and Gran looked eagerly around. She went straight to a rail of leather trousers.

"Oh these are wonderful. Just feel them Prune. They're so soft and look they've got loads. They're bound to have my size."

Mum's heart sank but she agreed the trousers felt very comfortable. "They're not very practical though are they," she said to Gran, but too late. Gran already had three different pairs of trousers hanging over her arm.

"I'll just try these on to begin with," she said to mum.

Mum looked at the price label. "Good grief!" she said.

After three quarters of an hour Gran got what she wanted: a small tan leather jacket and a soft pair of leather trousers in a "subtle green."

"Traffic light green if you ask me," mum said to Donna later.

At last Gran had cheered up and she didn't mind being hurried along to go and meet the others at Club Nautico. It was already 9 o'clock and mum led Gran through the now busy streets of St. Fernoux. People were sitting at outside cafes, eating and drinking and a small fun fair had started up by the beach.

"I don't think Spanish people go out until much later than we do," said mum. "Sounds good to me," said Gran.

They rounded the corner to the Club Nautico. It was transformed. Lots of seats and tables had been placed outside on the pavement and a temporary stage had been constructed. The road in front of the club was closed to traffic. There were coloured lights, bunting and best of all, pop music being played by a DJ on the stage. "This is better," said Gran.

"Oh dear," said mum.

They searched for Nora, Ethel, Winnie and Donna through the crowd. Eventually they found them at a long table. Everyone from the Hotel was there. Young Gary and his girlfriend were jigging to the music. Gran was not pleased to see the vicar and the Wainwrights but she perked up when Nora told her the club sold *Sidekick Splashes*.

"The waiters are very good. They all speak English," said Nora.

"Tonight is Open Night anyone who wants to do a turn on the stage can

have a go."

"Oh no," thought Gran.

"It's like Friday night at the Legion Club," said Basil Wainwright.

"It's good to see the locals enjoying themselves," said the vicar.

Gran sat down with her Sidekick Splash and her worst fears were realised when an elderly Spanish couple sang a dreary song while a man played an accordion.

"It's about the fish in the sea," said a waiter.

It didn't last forever though and pretty

soon the young DJ was back at his
mixing desk and thumping dance music
was echoing down the sea-front.

Everyone seemed to be enjoying
themselves. Mary Whitefleet, the vicar
and the Wainwrights were drinking hot
chocolate.

"Why don't you try something else?"
asked Wally Coulter. "What about that
fruit punch everyone else is drinking?"

The vicar looked at the other tables
where there were large jugs of a red
liquid with lots of oranges and peaches
floating in it.

"I'm told it's very good," said Basil Wainwright. "Lots of peaches, why don't we try it?" And he persuaded Betty, Mary Whitefleet and the vicar to share a jug with him. "Sangria, I believe it's called," he said.

"Has it got nice fruit in?" Mary Whitefleet asked the waiter.

"Oh yes lovely fruit," said the waiter "You'll like it."

The evening turned into night time. The DJ played dance music but every so often, he stopped, if some one wanted to sing a song on the stage.

Just after midnight Gran made her big entrance.

Suddenly there was an announcement in Spanish including the words 'Ace Ada from England.' Everyone looked up to see Gran bounce onto the stage in her Green leather trousers. She went to the young DJ's mixing desk. Bass music thumped out followed by a drum machine and suddenly Gran was rapping away in English.

"Yeah, OK," shouted the younger members of the crowd. "Yeah OK" they

shouted and they stood up and jumped

about to the music.

Gran did a rap she called 'Leather in Spain.' You couldn't pick out all the words but young Gary said he heard;

"Swing - your - leather - bum - at - Club - Nautico."

Gran went down a storm. Everyone cheered when she finished, even mum wasn't too embarrassed. She and Donna had decided to share a jug of the 'Spanish Fruit Juice'. The Gang and everyone else were in Spanish holiday mood.

After Gran's performance, the Spanish DJ thanked her in English and asked if

"any more of 'Our English Friends' would like to do a turn?"

To everyone's surprise Basil Wainwright stood up. "I'll sing a song," he said. "I'll do a turn," and Basil announced that he'd do 'Coming Round the Mountain.'

Mary Whitefleet said she knew that one and she'd join in. Not to be out done Betty Wainwright stood up and pulled the vicar up on stage with them.

"You've got a lubbly voice vicar, I'b herb you at church," stuttered Betty Wainwright.

The four of them made their way to the stage. On the way, Basil borrowed an old Spanish man's straw hat. He put it on backwards then undid his shirt to the waist and tied the tail in a knot around his rather podgy stomach.

Two Spanish men with an accordion and a guitar joined them on stage and after a few words they all launched into *"She'll be coming round the mountain ..."* the vicar waved his hands to the audience at the bit when you repeat "when she comes". The Spanish audience joined in echoing "when she

gums!"

The song went down a treat. When they finished the audience cheered, clapped and whistled. Even Gran was on her feet cheering. Betty Wainwright curtsied three times and Basil threw his borrowed Spanish hat high into the air.

When they sat down again Betty Wainwright's face suddenly turned to a frown. "There's no more Spanish fruit juice," she said looking at the empty jug on the table.

"Don't worry," said a passing waiter "I'll bring you one free, on the 'ouse for

your singing and dancing."

Mum and Donna showed the Spanish people how to do the 'Okee Kokee'.

The vicar, Mary Whitefleet and the Wainwrights had one more jug of Spanish fruit juice. Then suddenly Betty Wainwright announced loudly to Basil that she needed to go home.

"It's time to go Bashil. I need to go Bashil. NOW BASHIL!"

Betty Wainwright looked very pale as she stood up. Basil followed her and took her by the arm. They bumped into some tables and made their way up the

street bouncing from one lamppost to the next.

"I hope they make it" said the vicar, helping himself to more juice.

Gran did one more rap and the night finished at 3:30 in the morning when Club Nautico closed. The English crowd said goodbye to everyone six times then Gran suggested they all Conga in a line back to their hotel.

Off they went through the winding Spanish streets; a long Conga de Englesie.

Gran at the front Ethel at the back
and the vicar and Mary Whitefleet
carried along in the middle. They all
sang Gran's song;

"Ada's got new trousers
Ada's got new trousers
La la la, la la la la."

As they turned the corner into their
hotel two Spanish police men were
walking along the street. They looked at
the dancing line hopping and singing
into the Hotel Geriatrica.

"English!" said one of the Policemen.

Winnie Gets Steamed Up

The hotel breakfast room was very quiet next morning. In fact, not many people went for breakfast at all.

Mum had coffee and toast. She told me later it was a pity that she and the vicar and Mary Whitefleet and the Wainwrights had all caught a bit of a tummy bug for a couple of days. She said it was the rich Spanish food.

Even Winnie and Ethel slept in late and they both decided to have a quiet lazy day around the hotel. Winnie is not

very good at doing nothing and after a few lengths of the hotel swimming pool and ten minutes reading a book she got bored and went for a walk. At the back of the hotel, through a gate in a tall green hedge, Winnie found the hotel tennis courts. A path led from the courts towards the Town Centre, across some waste ground. Winnie took the path. She wished she had her basketball with her and she pretended she was bouncing a ball as she walked along. She hadn't gone far when she thought she heard the sound of a real basketball

and looked up to see a group of local Spanish boys playing on an open basket ball court.

Winnie stopped to watch the game. They weren't bad. One side was wearing baseball caps the others had nothing on their heads. This was the only way you could tell which side was which. The boys in caps were doing well. They scored 6 baskets as Winnie watched. It was then that Winnie noticed that there were only four on the side without hats. She also saw that they were starting to argue amongst

themselves because they were losing.

Five against four, that's not fair Winnie, said to herself and without thinking anymore shouted out to the lads.

"Oi! Five against four is not fair! Let me join in."

The boys looked at her, said something in Spanish and carried on.

Winnie shouted again. The boys stopped and looked at Winnie. "Give me the ball," she shouted. "Give me the ball" and she gestured with her hands. The boys looked at each other then the

one holding the ball shrugged his
shoulders and threw it rather hard at
Winnie. Winnie caught it, wincing. She
then proceeded to bounce the ball all
around the boys, under her legs and
spinning it backwards into her hands
before throwing it 10 metres straight
into the basket at one end of the court.
The Spanish boys stood with their
mouths open. Winnie held up five
fingers on one hand and four on the
other and pointed at herself.

"I'll play for these," Winnie said and
that's how she found herself on the side

with no hats.

Winnie's skill certainly helped the no hats side and after ten minutes she had scored five baskets and set up two other shots. The score was now 28 - 30. Winnie was getting very tired. It was hot and her late night out was taking its toll. Winnie needed to stop. "If I could even up the score I could leave with dignity," Winnie thought to herself. Next time I get the ball I'll try a long range overhand shot. The next second the ball was in her hands. She eyed up the basket took aim and threw the ball

high into the air. It sailed against the blue sky arriving and dipping straight into the net.

"Yes," shouted Winnie "30 -30. I really have to go now." Winnie started to leave as the boys all rushed up to her. They were saying things in Spanish trying to persuade her to stay. When they realised Winnie was determined to go they all started cheering and clapping. "Olé Winnie," they shouted and Winnie was given a bottle of water and a baseball cap.

The boys carried on their game as Winnie made her way back to the hotel. She drank most of the water and realised she was puffing rather hard.

"It's no good. I'm not as young as I used to be," Winnie said to herself. "I need some proper rest and relaxation."

Winnie was still thinking about this when she walked into the hotel and saw the sign 'Hotel Geriatrica Health and Beauty Parlour. Try our complete relaxation therapy; sauna-massage and mud therapy only 50 Euros...' "That's what I need," said Winnie and she went

straight in to the beauty parlour to find out about it. A nice young lady called Maria explained all about it.

"It's really good for you," she said. "It tones up your muscles. Makes you feel ten years younger."

That was enough for Winnie. "Count me in," she said. "When can I try it?"

"We have a vacancy in 15 minutes if you like," said Maria. "Sauna's are not very popular in Spain."

"Well I've never tried one before," said Winnie. "Will you tell me what to do?"

"Certainly," said Maria. "If you would

like to go and take a shower, then put on this bathrobe we'll get started."

"Winnie was shown into a changing room, where she was given a locker for her clothes. She showered with a special herbal gel and then made her way to the sauna room. It was made of wood and it smelt line a pine forest. Maria told her to stay in for a short while at first then to go back in for longer. "When you come out each time go straight to the cold shower room and stay there for about a minute then go back into the sauna one more time.

Then a cold shower again. After that it will be time for your mud treatment," she said.

Steamy room, cold shower. Winnie was beginning to have doubts. Maria smiled at her and handed her a large white towel. "When you get inside, hang your bathrobe on the hook and sit on your towel on one of the benches. Remember the higher the bench the hotter it gets." Maria opened the door and Winnie stepped inside. It was so hot it almost took her breath away. Winnie could see nothing - just steam.

Gradually, her eyes got used to the steam and she found a long wooden bench. Gingerly she took off her bathrobe and sat down on her towel. She felt silly at first but the steam whirled around her like a friendly blanket.

After about 5 minutes, Winnie felt her ears and toes getting hot. "Time to cool down," she said to herself and she slipped on her bathrobe to go to the shower. Under the shower she went. She pressed the button to release the cold water.

One, two, three.

"Jeepers creepers!" shouted Winnie, as the cold water hit her very hot body. After the first shock, it felt very good and Winnie remembered Maria's instructions. She made her way back into the sauna.

It was still hot and very steamy. Winnie could just make out three different benches going up like steps. What did Maria say? The higher you go, the hotter it gets? Winnie decided she should go to the top, so she climbed to the top bench. It was like a bed and

there was a wooden block to put your head on so Winnie decided to lie down. She put her bathrobe on the bench to make it softer and covered herself with her large white towel. The steam swirled around and she disappeared in the mist.

Lying in the hot steam, covered by the towel Winnie felt very comfortable. She started to think of her game of basketball with the local boys when her thoughts were interrupted by the sound of the door opening into the sauna. This was followed by two voices and one fat,

one thin white shape entering the steam room.

"What do we do then Wally?" said one voice. "I've never done this before. You said you'd tell me what to do."
"Oh it's easy," said the other voice.
"You just take your clothes off and sit here. Then you go for a shower."
"Well it might be easy but I can't see a thing in here."
"Just find a bench and sit on it Harry," said voice number two.

Winnie realised the voices belonged to Harry Thistlethwaite and Wally of

Wally's driving school. They were coming for a sauna. They hadn't seen her lying on the top bench and although Winnie was startled, she decided to lay still and say nothing.

"Now," said Wally "I'll just put some water on that stove thing to get a bit more steam."

Wally and Harry Thistlethwaite had spent the morning talking about cars, buses and engines when Wally said he liked to relax in a sauna after a long day at the wheel. Harry said he'd never tried it and Wally persuaded him to try

it out in the hotel fitness parlour.

As Wally put water on the stove,
Harry sat at one end of the bench with
his back to Winnie still in his white robe.

Wally went to the other end of the
bench. "Right take your kit off," he said,
slipping his robe off as he sat down.

"Feel a bit daft to be honest," said
Harry Thistlethwaite. "Still when in
Spain do as the Spaniards do." Harry
slipped out of his robe but stayed sitting
on the rest of it.

Winnie could see Harry had a tattoo
on the top of his right arm. 'Zoro 1000'

it said and it had a picture of a large spanner. Winnie had to bite her lip to stop herself laughing.

Harry and Wally sat in silence at opposite ends of the bench. Eventually Harry said something.

"How's your mother?" he asked.

"Doing well," said Wally.

"And your Aunt Doris?"

"Still in hospital, but recovering, thanks, said Wally. "What about your uncle Bob? Does he still grow them onions?"

"He does yeah! Gets um like cricket balls, ahh."

"Yes."

"Well then."

Harry and Wally sat in silence once more while Winnie bit her fingers. The sight of fat Harry Thistlethwaite and thin Wally of Wally's driving school sitting with nothing on, either end of a steamy bench was just too funny. She thought she was going to burst.

"You know Wally this is relaxing," said Harry. "But I'm not sure what my passengers would say if they could see me now."

"Probably hold tight, move along the

bus", said Winnie, as she suddenly burst out laughing.

"What the heck."

"Who's that?" said Wally.

"A woman! There's a blooming woman in here. Quick get out," said Harry Thistlethwaite. Wally and Harry grabbed their bathrobes and rushed for the door. They both tried to get out together and got stuck.

Through the steam Winnie saw four white cheeks squeezing through the door way. Hairy Harry and Wobbling Wally, thought Winnie, as she trembled with laughter.

She was still laughing after her final shower as she lay face down on a long massage bench. Maria wondered what made Winnie so happy, as she covered Winnie in dark, thick, browny-bluey mud.

"This mud is from the local hills." Maria explained to Winnie. "It's full of natural minerals; it does wonders for

your skin. Twenty minutes in this will make you ten years younger." Maria put mud all over Winnie just leaving gaps for her eyes, mouth and nose. When she had finished, she wrapped Winnie in a special sort of cling film, then wheeled her on the massage bench outside near to the swimming pool.

"Now just lay here in the shade and relax," said Maria and she moved a large sun shade so that Winnie was out of the sun. "We don't want to bake you," laughed Maria. "I'll come back in twenty minutes."

Winnie was still laughing quietly to herself. She felt wonderful. She was relaxed - the mud felt good. She had played basketball. She had tried the sauna. Winnie closed her eyes and went to sleep.

The sun was high in the sky. People near the pool were getting very hot. They were jostling to keep their sunshades to stay cool in the shade. Eight minutes into her snooze Winnie did not see a hairy tattooed arm reach for her sunshade and take it to the far end of the pool area.

Twelve minutes later Winnie was woken by Maria's startled voice.

"Oh my goodness! Oh dear!"

Winnie heard Maria's voice but she could do nothing. She couldn't move. The mud around her had baked solid in the hot sun. Winnie could hardly move her lips.

"Geh me ou!", shouted Winnie. "Get me ou!"

Winnie was stuck solidly inside the mud pack. Maria was panicking. She was tapping on the solid mud that covered Winnie's tummy. It made a

solid tapping noise like someone knocking on a door.

"Oh dear," said Maria, "Oh dear. Julietta, Rosa," she called. "Quickly, quickly, Winnie has been baked!"

Julietta and Rosa hurried out. Together with Maria they picked Winnie up like a stiff piece of wood and carried her indoors.

People around the pool area stopped and listened as they heard tapping and cracking noises mixed with cries from Winnie as Maria, Rosa and Julietta worked to force Winnie from her

cocoon.

After several hot showers Winnie was freed from the mud. Maria said she could have all of the treatment for nothing. Winnie cheered up when she realised she'd saved money and felt ten years younger.

My mum said Winnie "coped with it very well." There was only one sticky moment the next day when Gran asked her if she'd like a Bakewell tart for tea.

Ethel's Double Buggy

Just as everyone was beginning to relax the last day of the holiday arrived. Mum said how surprised she was that she'd really enjoyed it. Gran made two more visits to the Club Nautico and had swapped telephone numbers with Sebastian the Spanish DJ. Nora walked around the town as proud as punch wearing her Cost Bravo medal. The local boys, who knew what it meant, whistled and put their thumbs up to her. Winnie was busy making plans to

open her own health club when she got home 'For the more mature sporty woman.'

Everyone else said they had a good time as well. Even Basil and Betty Wainwright were chirpy and happy. They were even talking to Ethel, mostly "How are you's?" and "Good morning's" but this was a big change from the usual hostilities. In fact the Wainwrights and Ethel were getting on so well they agreed to share a taxi from the hotel to the far end of town.

Because it was the last day of the

holiday, most people were doing 'last minute things'; buying presents or souvenirs. Ethel told Gran at breakfast that she wanted to check out the local race track circuit that some one had told her about. "Just to have a look before I go home." She said it was at the south end of the town near a drinks warehouse called 'Sunny Sangria'. Basil Wainwright over-heard and said he wanted to go that way to buy some souvenirs and he suggested that Ethel share a taxi with him and Betty.

So, later that day Ethel, Basil and

Betty set off together. Basil and Betty in search of Spanish fruit drinks and Ethel in search of speed. They didn't say much to each other in the taxi. Ethel said she'd enjoyed the holiday but had missed tuning her engines. Betty coughed and frowned. They went through the main square of St. Fernoux along the road by the sea front and south towards the edge of the town, where the road climbs up into the hills. The taxi climbed the steep hill, past houses and shops built into the hillside. At one point Basil thought the taxi wouldn't make it up the hill but they made it to the top and pulled into the car park of 'Supermacardo Sunny Sangria - Drinks Warehouse'. Basil paid the taxi driver and he and Betty headed off into the 'Sunny Sangria.' "But where's the race track?" asked Ethel. "Sorry no English," said the taxi driver, "No English," and he drove away.

Ethel was left on her own in a large car park on top of a hill. She had a beautiful view of St. Fernoux and the sea and beaches but she did not have a race track. "This can't be right," she said to herself. "This is the middle of nowhere on top of a hill." She was just about to get really angry, when she saw two large lorries, slowly drive up the hill and into the large car park. She watched several young men jump out and start to unload wheels, frames and racing gear. Ethel was puzzled and excited. Something to do with racing was going on. Ethel spoke to a man in orange overalls. He said his name was Miguel. He spoke good English and he explained to Ethel that racing took place once a week but there was no race

track. The racing takes place on the main road starting in the car park of the Sunny Sangria and finishing in the main square of St. Fernoux. "The police close the road especially for the race," said the man. "Lots of people come to watch."

"But where are the racing cars?" asked Ethel.

"We do not race cars," said Miguel. "We race the carts - Spanish carts," and he pointed towards another man, who had nearly finished putting frames and wheels together. "They have no engine. We use the hill for our speed. We go very fast. It's very dangerous. You must come and see," said Miguel. "We start in three hours time. First we get ready."

Ethel couldn't believe it. She had seen racing carts made out of wooden boxes and pram wheels, the sort children build, but she had never seen carts like these. They had bright coloured steel frames, proper racing wheels, steering wheels, brakes, everything like a racing car except no engine.

Ethel thought about what Miguel had said. "The hill is our speed. The hill is our speed." She wanted to try it out

herself. She loves racing, she loves speed. Ethel asked Miguel about it. Anyone could enter the races and she told him about herself. At first Miguel looked puzzled and surprised but when Ethel showed him her English racing permit from her handbag he looked impressed.

"You cannot enter on your own," Miguel said. "You have no cart. But as a special treat to you, special lady, you can drive with me in the last race tonight. It's for double buggies - two seaters. You can drive and I'll be the brake and cornering man. You can be my partner. I'll lend you a crash helmet. See you here at 7 o'clock."

Ethel was so excited she kissed Miguel on both cheeks. "Yes! Yes!" she said "I'll see you here later," and without thinking about Betty and Basil, she took a taxi on her own, back to the hotel.

Mum saw Ethel come running into the Hotel. She went straight to Gran and told her about her race. Gran said it sounded wonderful and it would be a great way to finish off the holiday. She said she'd get everybody to go to the square to watch Ethel come down the hill.

"It can be our goodbye to St. Fernoux," said Gran.

Mum wasn't too sure.

Ethel was at the top of the hill long before 7 o'clock. Miguel met her with a smile, a pair of orange overalls and a bright blue crash helmet. "You won't need them until the last race - the double buggy. There are two single races first. Watch how the drivers lean into the bends as they go down hill. The trick is to keep the speed up at the top so you have enough left for the flatter, slower run into the town square at the bottom. Steer as close to each corner as you can. We don't want to end up in the sea Ethel," said Miguel with a laugh.

At the bottom of the hill the holiday gang was lost in a huge crowd of local Spanish people. The police had closed off the roads and were stood in their blue uniforms at various points down the long steep road from the top. At each bend down the hill, there were piles of straw bales and all the lamp posts by the side of the road were covered in soft protective plastic jackets. The finishing straight into the main square was lined with straw bales and old rubber tyres. Paper decorations and balloons were hanging everywhere. Thousands of people had come to watch. Gran recognised Sebastian the local DJ. He owned a house near the bottom of the hill near the square. Gran persuaded him that it would be a good idea if he invited her and her friends into his garden to watch the race.

Sebastian produced a ladder and everyone climbed up to the flat roof of his garage. They had a great view of the hill and the finishing straight.

Suddenly the crowd went quiet. A man said something over the loud speakers. Fireworks were let off and the whole crowd turned towards the top of the hill and shouted "trez, dos, uno." The first run had started.

Mum said she didn't like being on a garage roof so she stood behind Young Gary. As the carts in the first race came round the first bend at the top of the hill the crowd let out a great cheer. The carts whizzed around the bends, down the hill. They each had different coloured crash helmets. Mum said she could hear the scrunch of the wheels on the road and the rattle of the metal frames as they flew down the hill.

Half way down the hill a man in a yellow hat was well in the lead. "He's going too fast," said Young Gary. At the next bend he caught the side of a straw bale. He spun round and fell out of his cart. He rolled off the side of the road into someone's garden. His cart slid into the bales. At the next corner, two more people crashed into bales. Then a cart lost a wheel which flew threw the air onto the roof of a nearby restaurant.

"Good grief, this is dangerous stuff," said Harry Thistlethwaite. "If I drove my bus like that we'd all end up in hospital."

Half of the carts that had started were out of the race as those that remained, sped past Gran and the Gang. My mum closed her eyes.

The leading carts sped into the straight leading to the square. At the front was a blue helmeted driver, it was Miguel. He was speeding towards the finishing line. He crossed it first, then put the brakes on hard. Unfortunately he didn't stop in time and he ended up in the back of the tent selling candy floss. Two minutes later he emerged, covered in pink gunge and holding his arm. The crowd rushed towards him and put a green laurel leaf necklace around his neck. The crowd shouted "Olé Olé" and people in overalls threw sweets into the crowd. It was pandemonium.

Gran's English crowd on the garage
roof were speechless. They stood open
mouthed at what they had just seen.
Eventually Donna broke the silence.
"Ethel's never going to do THAT is
she?"

Back in the Sunny Sangria car park
Ethel was thinking exactly the same.
She'd never seen anything so
dangerous. Racing with engines has got
nothing on this she thought. Still Ethel
is a racer - it's in her blood and she was
going to give it a go.

The next race came and went, so did

two racers who were taken to hospital with cuts and bruises. The time of the last race, Ethel's race, was approaching. The teams were unloading the double buggies from the lorries. Ethel could see Miguel's team getting ready but she couldn't see Miguel. She went over to his double buggy and was helped into the driver's seat by the team. They pushed her to the far edge of the Sunny Sangria car park; the starting line. A few moments later Miguel came running towards her. He was holding his arm. "Accident Ethel," he said "I had an accident in the first race. My arm is bad. I really don't think I can ride with you Ethel. I'm so sorry, I'm so sorry."

Miguel took off his blue crash helmet and threw it onto the seat next to Ethel.

"I'm so sorry Ethel, I'm so sorry. I have to go to hospital." He turned to walk away and was helped into an ambulance by the rest of his team. Ethel was left sitting at the back of the start line all alone. At least she was until she heard three English voices.

Basil and Betty were coming out of The Drinks Warehouse. The Vicar had

joined them. He wanted to take some Spanish fruit juice home for the next church bazaar. They were looking for a taxi back to the hotel.

"Look it's Ethel," said Basil Wainwright.

"So it is," said the Vicar.

"Racing in Spain by the look of it," said Betty.

"Afraid not," said Ethel. "I nearly was, I've lost my co-driver and now I can't go on my own - it's a double buggy race."

"Doubles eh?" said Basil. "We've just had doubles in the Sunny Sangria -

lovely fruit juice."

Basil wobbled about a bit while he spoke.

"Doubles no troubles," he said to Ethel as he walked around to Ethel's spare seat. He picked up Miguel's crash helmet, threw it out of the car, and got into the spare seat alongside Ethel. "Doubles no troubles," he said again. "I can race in Spain. I'll race with you Ethel."

"Tres, dos, uno," shouted the crowd below. The starter dropped his flag and the teams pushed off their buggies, all

except Basil and Ethel, who were left
still at the start.

The vicar and Betty Wainwright
looked at the stationary double buggy.
They looked at the steep hill. They
looked at each other. Then without
saying a word they pushed Basil and
Ethel as hard as they could. Ethel and
Basil were racing down the hill.

Ethel was surprised to be moving and
already going fast. Straight away her
racing brain kicked into gear. She
steered a line for the first corner. On the
right hand side she could see the sea

way below her. To the left was the

mountain side...and Basil.

He was grasping the front of his seat

shouting "Go Ethel go! We're racing

down the mountain. Go Ethel go!"

The cart picked up more speed, as the hill became steeper. Way in front, the other carts had turned the next corner. Ethel could see the sea again and she was desperate not to nose dive into it. Her foot moved for the brake but it wasn't there. In fact Ethel's side of the cart had no peddles at all. The only thing she could control was the steering.

"I don't like this Basil," said Ethel. "There's no control on the thing. I'm just steering and hoping."

The car picked up even more speed. Ethel steered nearer to the mountain side.

Halfway down the hill, on top of the garage, Gran and the gang were watching the race. Wally Coulter was looking through his small pair of binoculars to see what was happening. "I can't see Ethel," he said to Gran. "Hang on, wait a minute, there she is right at the back, in the blue crash helmet and...and I don't believe it! She's got Basil Wainwright with her! Basil and Ethel are racing together!"

Gran snatched Wally's binoculars from him. She looked at the blue helmeted cart. "Saints preserve us," she said.

A buzz of excitement spread around the gang on the garage roof as they all realised Ethel and Basil were representing them in a cart race in Spain.

Faster and faster went Basil and Ethel. Basil was now singing "We'll be coming down the mountain when we come."

"Stop your singing you silly old buffer," shouted Ethel. "We need to

slow this thing down. The brake peddle is on your side. Put your foot on the brake."

"We don't need a break. I'm not tired" said Basil. "We've only just started."

Ethel concentrated hard on keeping the cart on the road. They were now going so fast the wind was taking her breath away. As they turned another bend the cart tilted on to two wheels going sideways. Ethel leaned with all her weight in the opposite direction to keep the cart upright. This caused Basil to fall forward and his foot hit the brake peddle for the first time. The cart moved sideways, Ethel could see they were heading straight for a large hotel at the side of the road. She steered the cart as well as she could and managed to head for a small gap between a straw bale and a Spanish policeman. He jumped out of the way. A thin Spanish cat ran up a tree. "Blooming cats," thought Ethel. She had driven into the drive way of the hotel but she still couldn't stop the cart. Fortunately the hotel drive way was dusty and it slowed them down a bit. Ethel headed for the exit. She managed to get the cart back onto the road going down the hill. In the distance, in the town square most of the other carts had crossed the finishing line. Ethel and Basil were now the only cart left coming down the hill. As they reached the garage by the gang everyone cheered.

"Go Ethel go," shouted Wally Coulter.

"Good old Basil," shouted Bob Yates.

"Go for the gang," shouted Winnie.

Basil was now singing even louder and the Spanish crowd could hear him. They realised they were watching two

elderly English people racing in a cart.
The crowd listened to Basil's singing
and decided to join in;

Basil   **Crowd**

"We are coming down the
mountain when we come,

                         Olé, Olé,

We are coming down the
mountain when we come,

                         Olé, Olé,

We are coming down the mountain,
coming down the mountain,
coming down the mountain
coz we can

Olé, Olé Olé,"

Ethel had driven the cart brilliantly
and had managed to slow it down. They
were now going at a safe speed, so she
decided to join in the fun. As Basil
sang, Ethel zig-zagged the cart from
side to side. They entered the town
square to singing and cheering. As they
crossed the finishing line sixteen
English people jumped for joy on the
garage roof belonging to Sebastian. This
was too much for the wooden supports
and they gave way. The roof tilted and

fell down. Winnie, Nora, Gran, my mum and all their friends were tipped fully clothed into Sebastian's swimming pool.

It took ages to get everyone dry and packed for the airport and the trip home. Betty and the vicar told everyone they were sorry they had missed the swimming pool party.

My mum got home in the early hours of the morning next day. She gave me some presents and made a cup of tea.

All about Gran's Gang

"Well," she said. "You wouldn't
believe what happened in Spain, on
holiday with your Gran
  And her Gang".

All about Gran's Gang

My Gran's got a gang. They all live
down our street and they're **trouble**.

My mum says she doesn't know
what to do. She's worried that Gran
will be 'put away' if she doesn't 'mend
her ways'.

Gran's good at mending things: socks,
jumpers and stuff like that. And she's
ever so good with wool.

She can knit anything you want but
I've never seen her 'mending her ways'.

Gran lives down the road at No. 52.
Next-door at 54 is Ethel. Across the road
at 61 is Winnie and next to her is Nora.

My Gran's name is Ada. *Ada, Nora,*

Winnie and *Ethel* that's Gran's gang.

Well, as I've said my Gran's good

at knitting but that's not all.

She performs in night clubs. She does

juggling, tells jokes and disco dances.

She stays out late. My mum says she

should 'retire gracefully' or 'get a proper

job'. Gran tells mum she's jealous and

that she should 'loosen up' or she'll

turn in to a prune. My mum hates

it when she's called a prune.

Once, mum got so angry she stormed

out of Gran's house and was nearly run

over by Ethel. Ethel was driving back

from the racetrack and didn't see mum.

You see, Ethel drives stock cars at the

local stadium and she's not a very

careful driver.

She builds the cars in her garage.

There's always lots of banging and

revving of engines. Sometimes there are

rude words as well when she hits her

fingers with a spanner.

Anyway, Ethel was returning from the *Demolition Derby* in her 'pride and joy' an old open top sports car and she just wasn't paying attention. Mum crossed her driveway and Ethel missed her by inches.

'*Unethical Ethel*', that's her racing name.

My mum says that Winnie is racy

but in a different way. Not just because

she races around a lot at basketball.

My mum says Winnie wears shorts

a lot just to flirt with the granddads

in our street. When she's not weaving

and dunking between the lampposts,

Winnie plays basketball in the local

Women's League. She plays centre

in the 'Silvergrey Goddess Giants'

(sponsored by Perma Wave hair

products).

Nora is Winnie's best mate and the

oldest member of the gang. She's also

the fattest which makes it very

dangerous when she's on her roller

blades. She's still got a part-time job

cleaning offices early in the mornings,

when no one's around.

That's when she roller

blades

to work.

My mum says Nora

roller blades down

the corridors of the

offices she cleans.

"At least she's away from the kids

there" says my mum.

"She's a menace on the pavement when

the kids are about."

There you are then, Ada, Nora, Winnie

and Ethel; Gran's gang. They're trouble.

What the Spanish Words Mean

Fiesta de belleza *Festival of beauty*

Atención *Attention, be careful, look out*

No paseo *No walking*

Plaza de héroe *Hero Square*

Número Uno *Number One*

Brillante *Brilliant*

Costa Bravo (gang) *Brave Coast Gang*

Geriatrica *old person*

Nautico *(From the) Sea*

Nino *Child*

Olé *well done*

Tres *Three*

Dos *Two*

Uno *One*

Adrian Townsend

Likes writing stories and going on holiday to Spain. He is married with two grown-up daughters. He likes watching football and Opera.

If you enjoyed this book look out for other stories by the same author including:

Powerful Eyes

and

Naughty Lessons

Gran's Gang will be causing more trouble soon.